BIG WORDS
small stories

THE
MISSING
DONUT

"I hope the whole book isn't like this page."

For my sprinklers, Isaac, Leni, Eleanor and Reis — J.H.

For my grandparents — T.L.M.

Text © 2018 Judith Henderson
Illustrations © 2018 Trenton McBeath

Kids Can Press gratefully acknowledges the financial support of the Government of Ontario, through the Ontario Media Development Corporation; the Ontario Arts Council; the Canada Council for the Arts; and the Government of Canada, through the CBF, for our publishing activity.

Published in Canada and the U.S. by Kids Can Press Ltd.
25 Dockside Drive, Toronto, ON M5A 0B5

Kids Can Press is a Corus Entertainment Inc. company

www.kidscanpress.com

The artwork in this book was rendered in graphite pencil and colored in Photoshop.
The text is set in Bizzle-Chizzle.

Edited by Yasemin Uçar
Designed by Julia Naimska

Printed and bound in Malaysia, in 3/2018 by Tien Wah Press (Pte) Ltd.

CM 18 0 9 8 7 6 5 4 3 2 1

FSC
www.fsc.org
MIX
Paper from responsible sources
FSC® C012700

Library and Archives Canada Cataloguing in Publication

Henderson, Judith
[Short stories. Selections]
    The Missing Donut / written by Judith Henderson ; illustrated by T. L. McBeth.

(Big words small stories)
Short stories.
ISBN 978-1-77138-788-0 (hardcover)

    1. Readers (Elementary). I. McBeth, T. L., illustrator II. Title.

PE1117.H46 2018   428.6'2   C2017-907006-1

BIG WORDS
small stories

THE MISSING DONUT

"Come on, Crat!"

Written by **Judith Henderson**

Illustrated by **T. L. McBeth**

KIDS CAN PRESS

Table of Contents

Who's Who

Meet Cris.
He likes things all
in a row.

Meet Crat.
He likes to mix
things up.

This is the
Sprinkle Fairy.

She has a word factory
in Sicily. That's where the
best words in the world
come from.

ITALY

Sicily

These are the Sprinklers. They're the Sprinkle Fairy's helpers.

They sprinkle Big Words into small places. If you happen to spot a Sprinkler in a story, it means there's a Big Word coming!

BIG WORD!

"Feel free to borrow the Big Words — no charge."

The Missing Donut

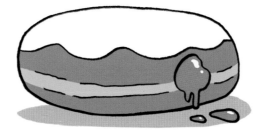

I was in the mood for a donut. My favorite kind is jelly.

There was supposed to be one left in the box. I know, because I left it there.

But when I opened the box ... nothing!

"Big Word coming. BIG!"

It had been purloined!

"PURLOINED!
Big Word! Big Word!"

Say it: purr-loynd

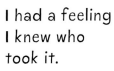

I had a feeling
I knew who
took it.

Tap
Tap
Tap

"Crat, did you
eat my last
donut?"

"You mean the yummy
one filled with
strawberry jelly?"

"Yes, that
one."

"Can't say."

"Can't say why?"

"Because ... ummm ...
It could have been the
Sprinkle Fairy? She
might have purloined
the donut."

"Ooooh, bad, bad kitty! I heard that! It's not nice to blame the Sprinkle Fairy."

"Yeah, you don't want to upset the Sprinkle Fairy. She could turn you into a hot dog again."

"Well, I didn't purloin the donut. And even if I did, I couldn't give it back."

"And why is that?"

"Because it's in my tummy."

13

PURLOINED is a Big
Word that means stolen.

It's All Downhill

"That's a nice new shiny red bike. Can I ride it?"

"No, you may not."

"Why not?"

"Because it's new."

"But I'm a master bike rider. A wizard of the wheels. What could go wrong?"

"A lot."

"Don't worry. I will go oh-so-slow — slower than a snail."

"Well ... okay."

"The brakes are here. If you go too fast, squeeze them to slow down. Remember that, okay?"

"Squeeze to slow. Got it — no biggie."

"Hi there ... Well, hello ... Nice day, isn't it? Like my shiny bike?"

"Nice bike, Crat.
But it sure is SLOW."

Slow? *Grr.*
I'll show her.

"Whee! Look at me!"

AHHHHHHHH.!!!!!

"The brakes!
Squeeze the brakes!
BRAKES!!!"

SCREEECH!

"I didn't know cats could fly."

"I thought you were a master — a wizard of the wheels!"

"CRAT! Did you hear me?"

"Big Word coming. BIG!"

"I can't answer right now. I'm feeling a bit ... discombobulated."

"DISCOMBOBULATED!

Big Word! Big Word!"

"Oh, *really*."

"He *must* be discombobulated. He tried to fly."

"Right after you fix my bike!"

"Yes. I'm very confused. I'm going to need a rest and a nice cup of hot chocolate."

DISCOMBOBULATED is a
Big Word that means confused.

The Trouble
with Chipmunks

Crat and I were just hanging around, when ...

"Uh-oh."

"Chipmunks."

Whisper Whisper Whisper

"Hello there. What are you two up to?"

"We're enjoying a little rest and relaxation."

"Ah yes, R and R. Can I interest you in a nut?"

"I wouldn't mind one."

"Okay, me, too."

"Take as many
as you like."

"Well ... gotta go. Don't forget
your sunscreen!"

"Can you turn up the radio? I can't hear anything."

"Uh-oh. Big Word coming!"

"It's gone! The radio's gone! We've been bamboozled!"

"BAMBOOZLED!
Big Word! Big Word!"

"Those good-for-nothing ..."

"Shh. Do you hear that?"

"Hello, Sprinkle Fairy.
May we help you?"

"Bamboozling is
against the law."

"Turn them into
hot dogs!"

"No, not hot dogs!"

"Um ... Can we interest you in a fresh nut instead?"

"No thanks."

BAMBOOZLED is a Big Word
that means to be tricked by somebody.

Museum of Fabulous Art

"And here we have a wonderful sculpture by Mr. Puffinpiece ..."

Puffinpiece

"It just looks like a balloon animal to me. I could do that."

"Just saying."

Shhhhh!!!

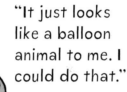

"Huh. It's hard as rock. I thought it was a balloon."

Poke!

Puffinpiece

"Crat! Be careful!"

33

"I need one of those in a hurry."

"Of course. Would you like a dog?"

"Anything. Just be quick about it, please."

"How about one that looks like you?"

"Me?"

"Wow, I look great."

"Oooh ... a Puffinpiece. Wonderful."

"And here we have a Puffin —"

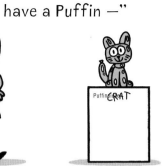

"PuffinCRAT?! What in the world ...? Where is the Puffinpiece?"

"Let's go."

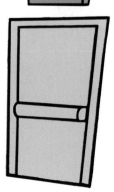

SMITHEREENS is a Big Word
that means little broken pieces.

Mr. Footz's Fine Footwear

It was a rainy day.

"Let's go for a walk."

"No thanks. I don't want to get my feet wet."

"You can put on your balloon booties."

"I'm not wearing balloons."

"What's wrong with balloons?"

"It's coming! Big Word coming!"

"I want *galoshes* like yours. Yellow ones."

"GALOSHES!
Big Word! Big Word!"

"But cats and dogs wear balloon booties."

"Well, I want GALOSHES."

"Okay, okay. Maybe Mr. Footz has cat galoshes."

Mr. Footz's
Fine Footwear

41

"Hello, Mr. Footz. We're looking for galoshes for Crat."

"I do not want balloons."

"Balloon booties would be better."

"There are no refunds on cat galoshes."

"In other words, you can't bring them back if you don't like them."

"Four yellow galoshes-es please."

"Wheeeeee!"

"I told you so."

"Now what am I going to do with these galoshes?"

"I'll take two."

GALOSHES is a Big Word that means rubber overshoes or boots for walking in the rain.

"Um ... um ... I am quite DISCOMBOBULATED! Can you tell by how confused I look?"

"Oh, yes, you do look confused. It must be because you were BAMBOOZLED."

"Yes, we heard that someone PURLOINED your delicious chocolate chip cookie. Let's go find who did it!"

"AHA! A clue! It's the footprints of tiny GALOSHES. And a trail of crumbs and chocolate chips!"

"Follow the delicious chocolate chip cookie SMITHEREENS!"

"CRA-AT!!!"

"Yes, yes. It was I, Crat, who BAMBOOZLED you."

"I PURLOINED the delicious chocolate chip cookie while wearing my GALOSHES."

"But the cookie broke into SMITHEREENS, causing me to be so DISCOMBOBULATED with worry that ..."

"I ate the whole thing."

The End.

Acknowledgments

To Yasemin Uçar (Yasey!), my editor — so lucky this project found you. No words **BIG** enough to thank you.
To my children — I totally lucked out.
And Cassy — for your head and heart.

— Judith Henderson

"ACKNOWLEDGMENTS!
Big Word! Big Word!"